D1096596

This book belongs to

....

First published in 2020 by Miles Kelly Publishing Ltd
Harding's Barn, Bardfield End Green, Thaxted, Essex, CM6 3PX, UK

2 4 6 8 10 9 7 5 3 1

Publishing Director Belinda Gallagher
Creative Director Jo Cowan
Editorial Director Rosie Neave
Senior Designer Rob Hale
Image Manager Liberty Newton
Production Elizabeth Collins, Jennifer Brunwin-Jones
Reprographics Stephan Davis
Assets Lorraine King

Cover Illustrator Monika Filipina

ISBN 978-1-78989-071-6

Printed in China

British Library Cataloguing-in-Publication Data
A catalogue record for this book is available from the British Library

Made with paper from a sustainable forest

www.mileskelly.net

My First Book of
Animal
Stories

Miles Kelly

Contents

The Hare and the Tortoise

The hare was always boasting about how fast he could run. "I'm the fastest in the land," he would say.

One day the hare said, "Which of you will run a race against me?"

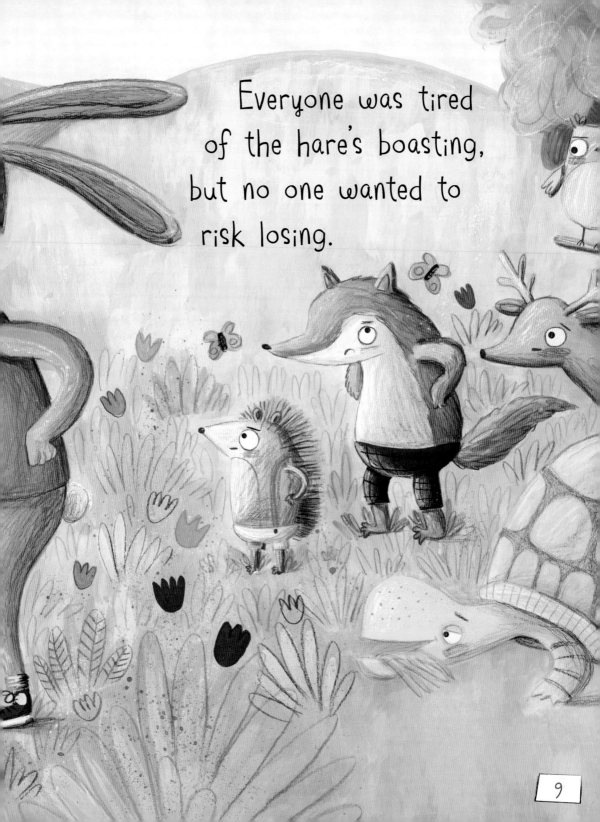

Everyone was tired
of the hare's boasting,
but no one wanted to
risk losing.

No one — except for the tortoise.

The hare laughed out loud, and all the other animals gasped. But the tortoise just smiled.

Preparations began. The fox drew up a map of the route. The race was to take place the following week.

For the next seven days the hare showed off, speeding around the meadow, dashing up hills and knocking animals over.

He upset just about everyone!
The tortoise watched from afar
as he chewed leisurely on grass
and leaves.

WHOOSH!

The evening before the race, the tortoise decided to have an early night. He settled down in his cosy bed just as the sun was setting.

"Early to bed and early to rise," said the tortoise to himself.

17

SHHH!

But the
hare stayed up late
partying with his neighbours,
the badgers. Their noisy
antics kept everyone awake.

The next day dawned bright and sunny. The tortoise awoke refreshed and full of energy. He ate a hearty breakfast, then got ready for the race.

The hare wasn't feeling quite so refreshed. His late night meant he had hardly slept at all. He felt exhausted.

He poured himself a large glass of carrot juice and yawned loudly.

23

Out in the meadow, the animals were gathering to watch the start of the race. Stalls were selling cakes and sandwiches.

Brightly coloured balloons and bunting had been tied to trees. A party atmosphere was building!

Feeling more like his usual self,
the hare took his place at the
start line.

"Get ready to lose!" he smirked to the tortoise. The tortoise just smiled.

Then the fox began the countdown to the race. "On your marks... Get set..." The whistle blew, and they were off!

The hare dashed away at full speed, around the meadow then up the hill. He stopped to look back and saw the tortoise plodding along far behind.

Grinning happily, the hare danced a little jig on the hilltop.

"YUMMY!"

Then the hare started to feel hungry. He grabbed two lettuces from a field and sat down to eat.

The sun was warm, so the hare settled down for a short nap. After all, he'd had a late night, and the tortoise was far behind.

All the while, the tortoise kept going. He plodded up and over the hill.

ZZZZZZ!

He saw the hare snoozing
under a tree, and marched
bravely past. The hare didn't stir
a whisker.

34

Much, much later, feeling stiff and cold, the hare woke up with a start.

He looked up at the sun and saw how low it was in the sky. It must be almost evening! He feared the worst.

The hare flew around the rest of the route at top speed. He ran like he'd never run before.

In the distance he heard shouting and clapping. The tortoise was nearly at the finish line.

PANT!

WHEEZE!

The tortoise was very tired. But with all the animals cheering and clapping, he staggered on, as fast as his legs would go.

He crossed the line to huge applause and the crowd shouting his name.

The hare had lost his own
challenge. From now on perhaps
he wouldn't be so boastful.
    Slow and steady wins the race.

How the Camel got his Hump

In the beginning of years, there was a camel. He lived in the middle of the Howling Desert and was most idle.

The camel didn't want to work like the other animals. When anybody spoke to him he would only reply...

"Humph!"

On Monday the horse went to see the camel. The horse had a saddle on his back and a bit in his mouth.

He said, "Camel, come out and trot like the rest of us."

"Humph!" said the camel.

And the horse went away and told the man.

On Tuesday the dog went to see the camel. The dog had a stick in his mouth.

He said, "Camel, come and fetch like the rest of us."

"Humph!" said the camel. And the dog went away and told the man.

On Wednesday the ox went
to see the camel. The ox had
a yoke on his neck. He said,
"Camel, come and
plough like the
rest of us."

"Humph!"

said the camel.
And the ox went away
and told the man.

That evening the man called the
horse and the dog and the ox
together.
"That camel in the
desert won't
work," he said.

"You three must work double to make up for it."

51

That made the horse and the dog and the ox very angry. So they held a pow-wow on the edge of the desert.

The idle camel strolled by and laughed at them.
Then he said, "Humph!" and went away again.

So the three animals went
to visit the genie in charge of
all deserts.

"An animal in the middle of
your Howling Desert is idle and
won't work," said the horse.

"That's my camel!" said the genie in surprise. "What does he say about it?"
"He says 'Humph!'" said the ox.

The genie flew off at once.

The genie found the camel being idle. "Camel, what's this I hear of you doing no work?" he asked.

"Humph!" said the camel. So the genie began to think a great magic.

"Everyone has had extra work since Monday, all on account of your idleness," the genie went on.

"Humph!" said the camel again.

So the genie went on thinking a great magic.

"I wouldn't say that again
if I were you," said the genie.
"You might say it once too
often. Camel, you must work."

But the camel only said

"Humph!" once more.

As soon as he said it, the camel's back began puffing up into a great big humph!

"There!" said the genie. "That's your very own humph that you've brought upon your very own self by not working."

The camel was horrified.
"You would not work for three days," the genie went on. "So your new humph lets you work for three days without stopping to eat or rest."

So the camel went away from the Howling Desert. And from that day the camel has had a humph, but we call it a hump now, to spare his feelings.

But he has never yet caught up with the three days of work that he missed at the beginning of the world.

And he has never yet learned
how to behave.

PUSS in Boots

There was once a miller who had three sons. When he died, he left the mill to his eldest son. He left a donkey to his middle son.

The youngest son was given
the miller's cat. "What am I to
do with a cat?" he said.
     But Puss replied, "Give me
some boots and a bag and
you shall see!"

So the youngest son gave Puss some boots and a bag. Puss put carrots in the bag. Then he hid in some tall grass.

Soon a rabbit came along and, tempted by the carrots, hopped into the bag.

Off Puss ran to the palace. He offered the rabbit to the king, saying it was a gift from the Marquis of Carabas.

The king was delighted. He thought the marquis must be very grand to have a cat who wore such fine footwear.

The next day, Puss said to the miller's son, "Come to the river and help me fish."

"HELP!"

Puss knew the king would
soon drive by in his carriage.
"Get into the water!" he told his
master. The miller's son did as he
was told. Then Puss hid his
master's clothes.

"STOP!" cried Puss, and he ran in front of the carriage. "My master, the Marquis of Carabas, has been robbed! Thieves stole his clothes as he swam in the river!"

The king ordered clothes to
be brought for the miller's son.
Then the king invited the miller's
son to ride in his carriage with
him and his daughter. Puss ran
off ahead.

Next, Puss met some workers gathering hay in the fields.

"When the king drives by, he will ask who owns this land," said Puss. "Say it belongs to the Marquis of Carabas."

Sure enough, the workers did as Puss had asked. The king was most impressed.

BANG! BANG!

Puss ran on ahead again. He came to a big castle where he knew an ogre lived. Puss knocked loudly at the gate and a servant let him in.

Puss was taken to meet the ogre, and he bowed down low. "What do you want?" the ogre growled.

Puss was scared, but he said, "I've heard you can do amazing magic Mr Ogre, and turn yourself into any animal. Can you turn into a lion?"

The ogre immediately became a fierce lion.

87

"It must be easy to turn into a big animal," said Puss. "But could you turn into... a mouse?" The ogre did just that. At once Puss POUNCED! And that was the end of the ogre.

SQUEAK!

Then Puss heard the carriage
approaching. He told the castle
servants to prepare a feast.

Then Puss rushed outside to
meet his master and the king.

"HELLO!"

The king stepped out of the
carriage, amazed.

"Welcome to the castle of the
Marquis of Carabas!" said Puss,
bowing low.

They went into the castle, where they all sat down to a most delicious feast.

The miller's son and the princess were getting on well. They talked and laughed together a lot.

The miller's son made the castle his home, and was a good and kind master to the servants.

And just one year later, he married the princess.

"Congratulations!"

Puss was very pleased at the way his plan had worked out.

The Ant and the Grasshopper

It was a warm, sunny summer's day. A grasshopper was hopping about in a field, chirping and singing very loudly.

Every day the grasshopper
danced, played music and ate to
his heart's content.

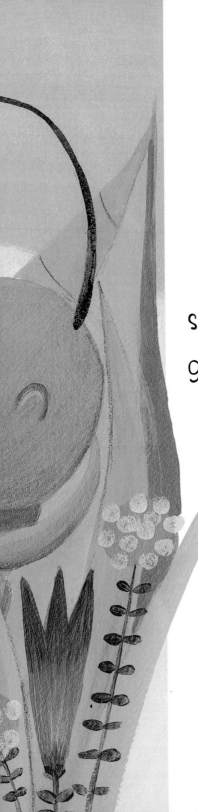

ZZZZZ!

After a morning of
singing and dancing, the
grasshopper started to
feel tired. He lay
back on a leaf,
dozing in the sun.

Huff!
Puff!

On the ground below
the sleeping grasshopper,
an ant was hard at work.

The ant's huffing and puffing woke the grasshopper.

"You should be resting and enjoying yourself, like me!" the grasshopper said to the ant.

"I need to get my food stored and my nest ready for winter," the ant replied.

"Winter isn't for months," laughed the grasshopper. "Come and sing and play and eat and rest with me."

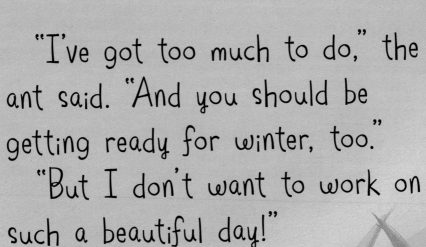

"I've got too much to do," the ant said. "And you should be getting ready for winter, too."

"But I don't want to work on such a beautiful day!" replied the grasshopper.

110

So the grasshopper kept playing. He sang songs and danced in the field.

He slept in the sunshine and ate lots of food.

The ant
continued to work,
storing food and
making his nest
warm and cosy
for winter.

In no time at all, the sunshine disappeared and the weather turned cold. The field was soon covered in a layer of frosty white snow.

Winter had arrived!

The ant was ready. While the snowflakes fell outside, the fire crackled inside his little nest.

Crackle!

He had enough food set by
that he wouldn't have to go
outside in the cold months ahead.

The grasshopper was very hungry, but he could not find any food. There was nowhere to shelter from the falling snow and bitter winds.

Then the grasshopper came
to the ant's house, and knocked
at the door.

He asked
the ant if he
had any food
to spare.

121

"Why don't you have any food of your own?" asked the ant. "Did you not store any in the summer? What were you doing?"

"I was so busy dancing and singing and eating... I didn't do any work at all!" said the grasshopper.

The grasshopper looked truly sorry. He promised the ant he would work hard next summer and store his own food.

So the ant gave him as much food as he could spare.

It was just enough to see the grasshopper through the winter, but it was a miserable few months for him.

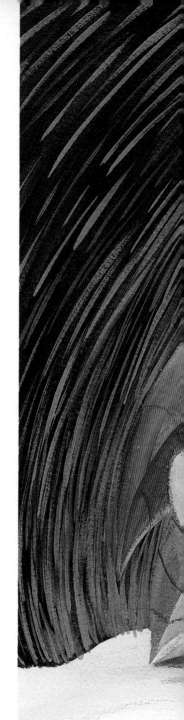

Next summer, the grasshopper was as good as his word. He worked hard to store enough food for himself.

The grasshopper even found time to help the ant, to thank him for sharing his food.

The next winter came and the grasshopper did not go hungry. He had learned that there is a time for work and a time for play.

How the Leopard got his Spots

There was once a leopard who had a yellowish-brownish coat. Everything around him — the grass, the rocks, and all the other animals — were a yellowish-brownish colour too.

The leopard was hardest to spot, so it was easy for him to sneak up on the other animals and eat them for dinner!

Sometimes the leopard hunted with his friend the man, and then the other animals didn't know which way to jump!

"Yikes!"

So bit by bit (the giraffe began it, because his legs were the longest) the animals scuttled off to find a place to hide.

At last they came to
a great forest. Trees
and bushes cast
stripy, speckly
shadows.

136

After a long time
of standing with the
slippery, slidy shadows
falling on them...

138

...the giraffe grew blotchy and the zebra grew stripy and the antelope grew darker.

At last you could hear them and smell them, but you could hardly see them at all.

Meanwhile, the leopard and the man could find nothing to eat except beetles and rats. Then they both had terrible tummyache!

"Ouch!"

So the leopard and the man went to see the wise baboon.

"Your breakfast has gone into other spots," the baboon told the leopard, "and you should do the same."

Then the baboon turned to the man. "Your breakfast decided it was time for a change," he said. "So you should change, too."

So the leopard and the man set off to look for

their breakfast. At last they came to a great forest, full of spotty, dotty shadows.

"What is this?" asked the leopard. "I can hear zebra. I can

smell zebra. But I can't see zebra."

"It's strange," agreed the man. "I can hear giraffe. I can smell giraffe. But I can't see giraffe."

That night, the leopard heard something moving in the dark, so he jumped on top of it. It felt like zebra. It smelled like zebra.

He heard the man catch something too. They decided to sit on these strange, invisible things until morning.

In the morning they looked at what they had caught.

Gasp!

The man said, "Mine looks like giraffe, but it is covered with brown blotches."

The leopard said, "Mine looks like zebra, but it is covered with black stripes. What have you been doing zebra?"

"Let us up," said the zebra, "and we'll show you."

So they did. The zebra walked to some bushes where the sunlight fell all stripy. Then the giraffe walked to some trees where the shadows fell all blotchy.

"Now, where's your breakfast?"

The leopard and the man looked, but they could see only stripy, blotchy shadows. "That's a trick worth learning," said the leopard.

"The trouble is, we don't match our backgrounds," said the man. "The baboon told me to change, so I'm going to change my skin." So he changed his skin there and then.

"But what about me?" asked
the leopard.
    "He told you to go into
spots," replied the man.
    "I wouldn't want silly
spots like giraffe," said
the leopard, with a shudder.

"Well you can't stay as you are," said the man. "You stand out in this forest like a lily in an ink pot!"

The leopard agreed. So the man put his fingers close together and pressed them on the leopard's fur.

Wherever his fingers touched they left five little marks, close together.

And you can still see them today on any leopard's skin you like.

"Now look at you!" said the man. "You can lie on bare ground and look like pebbles. You can lie on a branch and look like sunshine through the leaves. You

can lie right across a path and
look like nothing in particular.
Those animals will never see
you coming!"

The leopard lived happily
ever after, and
that is all!
Purrrr!

158

The Three Little Pigs

Once there were three little pigs who lived happily with their mother.

One day the three set off
to make their own way in
the world.

"Goodbye"

161

The three little pigs hadn't gone far when they decided to stop for a picnic. "Where are we going to live?" the little girl pig asked her brothers.

Then one of the little pigs saw a farmer with a cartload of straw. "Perfect house-building material," said the little pig, and he bought the whole load.

165

The little pig soon built his straw house. Suddenly a voice outside said, "Let me in, little pig." It was a big bad wolf!
"Not by the hair on my chinny chin chin!" replied the little pig.

"Then I'll huff and
I'll puff and I'll BLOW
your house down!"

The wolf blew down the house
of straw, but the little pig
managed to escape.

The two other little pigs carried on their way, until they met a woman with a huge load of sticks. The second little pig bought the sticks and built a house.

Then along came the big bad wolf. He knocked on the door of the stick house, and said,

"Let me in, little pig, let me in!"

But the second little pig said,

"Not by the hair on
my chinny chin chin!"

"Then I'll huff and I'll puff and I'll BLOW your house down!"

said the wolf. The stick house was soon just a pile of twigs.

The second little pig just had time to escape. He trotted off as fast as he could to look for his brother and sister.

Now, the third little pig had bought a load of bricks, and set about building a strong and sturdy house.

175

She worked very hard, and soon the house was ready. It even had a little garden and a chimney!

"Home sweet home!"

The third little pig settled into her new home. Then there was a knock at the door. It was her brothers!

Bang!

Bang!

They told their sister about
the big bad wolf. Together the
three little pigs hatched a plan.

Soon there was a loud
knocking at the door.
It was the big
bad wolf.

"Little pigs, little pigs, let me in!"

"Not by the hair on our chinny chin chins!" said the three little pigs.

"Then I'll huff and I'll puff and I'll BLOW your house down!"

And the wolf huffed and puffed... and puffed and huffed.

But the brick house was strong.
Inside, the little pigs put a big
pot of water on the fire to boil.

"You won't escape!" called the wolf, as he clambered onto the roof. He began to climb down the chimney.

But the little pigs were ready for him. The huge pot of water in the fireplace was very hot.

Suddenly there was a huge SPLASH as the wolf fell into the pot of water.

Splish! Splash! Splosh!

Boiling hot and very wet, the wolf ran away as fast as his legs could carry him.

"Hurrah!"

And the three little pigs
lived happily ever after in the
house of bricks.

How the Whale got his Throat

Once upon a time there was a whale, and he ate fish. He ate the starfish and the garfish and the crab and the dab...

...and the plaice and the dace and the really truly twirly-whirly eel. He ate all the fish he could find in all the sea.

One day the whale said, "I'm hungry."

There was now only one fish left in all the sea. The little fish said, "Noble whale, have you ever tasted man?"

"No," said the whale. "What is it like?"

"Nice," said the fish. "Nice but nubbly."

"Then fetch me some," boomed the whale.

"One at a time is enough," said the clever fish. And he told the whale where he could find a man.

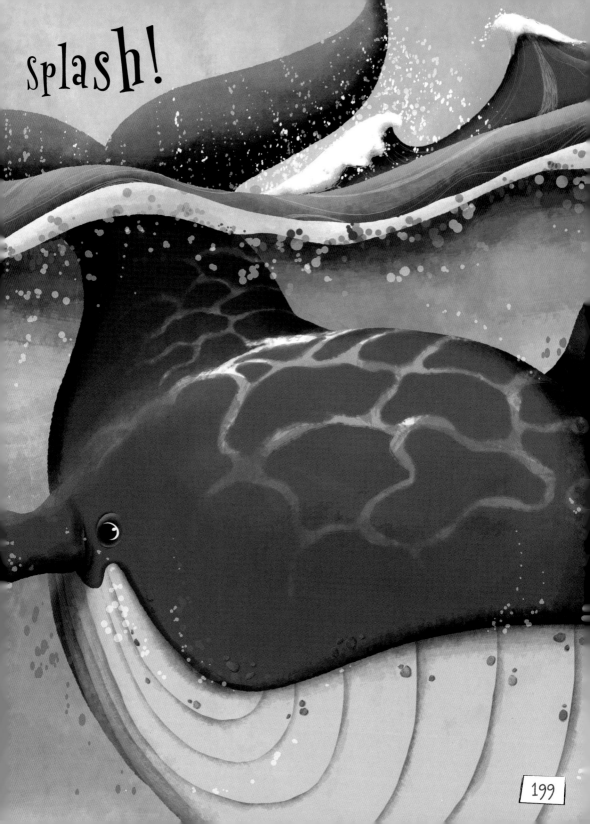

splash!

199

So the whale swam and swam, until he came to a raft in the middle of the sea. On the raft was a solitary shipwrecked sailor.

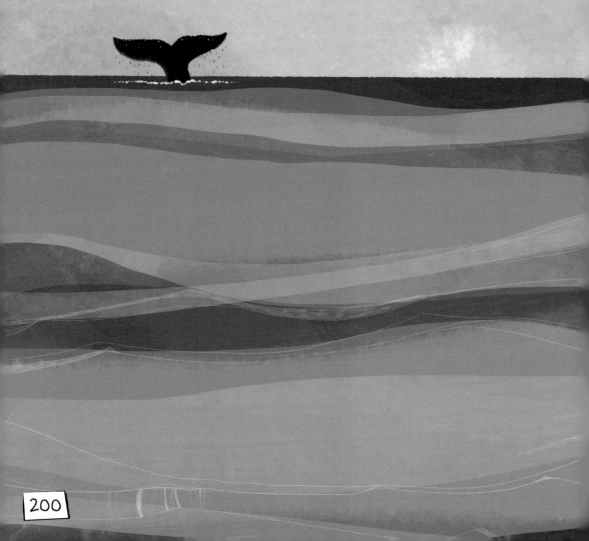

The sailor was trailing his toes in the water. All he had in the world were the clothes on his back, and a knife.

The whale opened his mouth
back and back and back, and
he swallowed the sailor,
and his clothes, and
his raft, and
his knife.

Gulp!

He swallowed them all down into his warm, dark, inside cupboards. Then he smacked his lips, and turned round three times on his tail.

But when the sailor found
himself inside the whale's warm,
dark, inside cupboards he
thumped and he bumped, and he
stumped and he jumped, and he

hit and he bit, and he banged and he clanged, and he hopped and he dropped, and he prowled and he howled, and he danced hornpipes where he shouldn't.

At this, the whale felt most unhappy. He said to the clever little fish, "This man is very nubbly, and he is making me hiccup. What shall I do?"

"Tell him to come out," said the little fish.

Hic!

So the whale called down his
own throat, "I've got hiccups!
Come out and behave yourself!"
"No!" said the sailor.
"Take me home, and
I'll think about it."
And he danced
even more.

"Well then, you had better take him home," said the clever little fish.

So the whale swam and swam and swam as hard as he could with his hiccups.

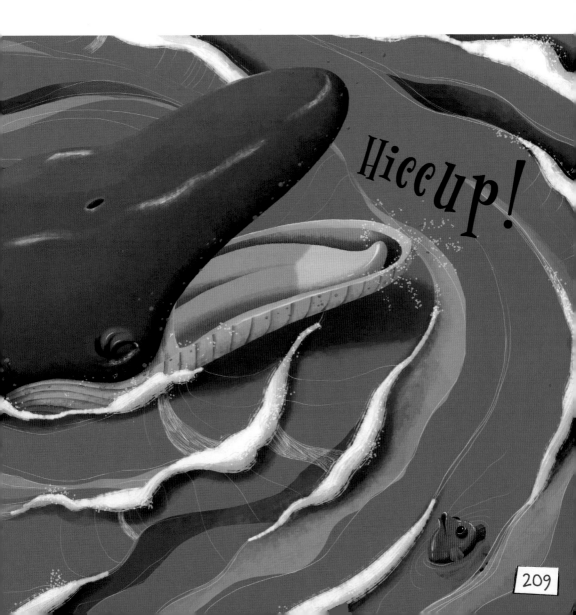

Hiccup!

While the whale was swimming, the sailor took his knife and cut up his raft to make a little square grating all running criss-cross.

He tied it firm with his braces.

211

And he wedged that
grating good and tight
into the whale's throat,
and there it stuck!

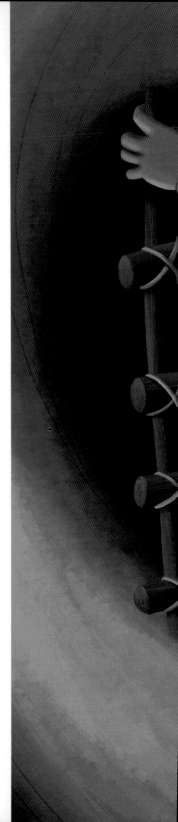

At last the whale saw the shore and he rushed halfway up the beach. He opened his mouth wide and wide and wide, and said, "We're at your stop, it's time to go!"

The sailor stepped out, waved goodbye to the whale, and went home — where he married and lived happily ever after.

As he went, he sang:
"By means of a grating
I've stopped your 'ating."

The clever little fish went and hid himself in the mud just under the door of the equator.

"Shhhhh!"

He was afraid that the whale
might be angry with him.

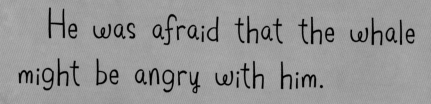

The whale
didn't find him
until he got out of his temper,
and then they were friends again.

From that day on, the grating in the whale's throat, which he could not cough up nor swallow down, stopped him eating anything except very, very small fish.

The starfish and the garfish
and the crab and the dab and all
the others were most relieved.

And that is the reason why whales today never eat sailors, or little boys or girls.

The Ugly Duckling

On a sunny spring day, when the countryside was covered in blossom, a duck sat on her nest on the riverbank.

At last, the shell of one egg began to crack. Then another, and then another.

"Peep, peep!" chirped the little ducklings.
"Quack, quack!" said mother duck.

"Oh dear, there's one egg left," mother duck sighed.

She settled back down on
the nest to wait.

A few days later, the big egg cracked, and the new duckling tumbled out. He was large, and grey, and looked rather strange.

"Peep!"

Mother duck was surprised. "But never mind," she quacked. "I shall treat him just the same as the rest."

The next day, mother duck led her family to the river. One by one the ducklings followed their mum into the water and their legs started paddling away.

Splish!

Splash!

Splosh!

Even the big, strange grey one
was swimming smoothly.
"Follow me," said mother duck.

"Quack quack!"

Mother duck hopped out of the river into the duck yard and the other ducks saw the big grey duckling.

"What is that ugly-looking thing?" they hissed. "We don't want him around here."

Mother duck tried to protect her strange little one, but they all said he didn't belong in the duck yard.

Every day, the ugly duckling was pushed about and made fun of by the other ducks. Even his brothers and sisters began to be nasty to him.

So one day the ugly duckling ran away. He sprang up into the air and dropped over the fence.

237

The ugly duckling ran until he reached a marsh. The wild ducks there all agreed that he was terribly ugly, but they said he could stay.

"As long as you keep your distance!"

He spent his days swimming on the marsh and looking for food. For weeks, no one spoke to him and no one cared about him. He was very lonely.

One evening, a flock of birds appeared. They were dazzling white, with long graceful necks.
The duckling crouched in the reeds, watching. He thought they were beautiful.

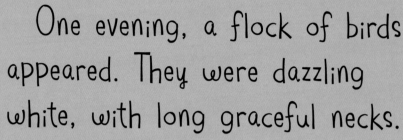

242

When they soared up into the sky, the duckling watched them go. He longed to be flying with them.

Winter arrived, and the marsh became so icy that the duckling very nearly froze.

The thought of seeing those magnificent birds again kept him going.

BRRRRRRR!

245

246

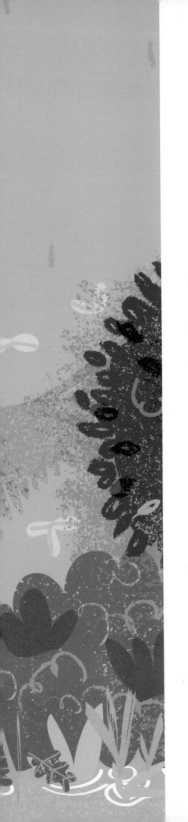

Then one day, spring
arrived. The sun shone,
and flowers opened
their petals to it.

The ugly duckling felt
strong. He stretched his
wings, gave them a
flap, and found himself
soaring into the air.

When he saw a river by a beautiful garden, he decided to have a swim.

Then he noticed three of
those white birds that he had
seen before the winter.

The birds swam towards the ugly duckling. Thinking that they would call him names, the ugly duckling looked down, nervously – and what did he see reflected in the water?

He was no longer clumsy and grey. He was dazzling white, with a long graceful neck.

"Hello!" said the graceful birds.

Then two children came into the garden. "Look, there's a beautiful new swan!"

The fourth swan held his head high. He had never dreamed that he would be this happy, back when he was an ugly duckling.

The ELEPhant's Child

In the far-off times the elephant had no trunk — only a bulgy nose as big as a boot. He could wiggle it from side to side, but he couldn't pick anything up with it.

But there was one elephant's child who was full of 'satiable curtiosity.

That means he asked EVER so many questions.

"But why?"

He asked his uncle the giraffe what made his skin spotty, and his uncle snorted down his snout. He asked his uncle the baboon why his face was flat, and his uncle poked him with his paw.

He asked his aunt the hippo
why her eyes were red, and his
aunt splashed him with her hoof.
But still he was full of
'satiable curtiosity!

"What does the crocodile have for dinner?" asked the elephant's child one day.

But his family just said, "HUSH!"

So he asked the kolokolo bird, "What does the crocodile have for dinner?"

"Go to the banks of the great grey-green, greasy Limpopo River," said the bird.

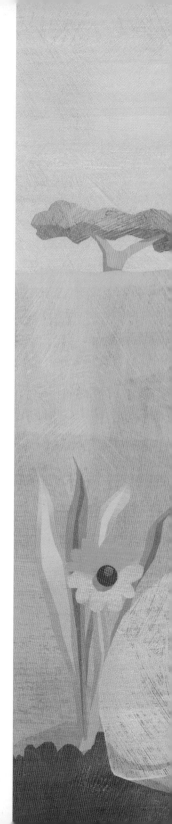

"Then you
can ask him
yourself!"

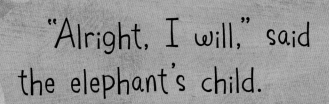

"Alright, I will," said
the elephant's child.

So the next morning,
the 'satiable elephant's
child set off to find
the great grey-green,
greasy Limpopo
River.

"Goodbye!"

The 'satiable elephant's child
had never seen a crocodile
before, so he did not know what
one was like.

The first creature he found
was a bi-coloured-python-rock-

snake, curled round a rock.

"'Scuse me," said the elephant's child. "Have you seen a crocodile anywhere? And could you tell me what he has for dinner?"

But the snake only shook his scalesome, flailsome tail.

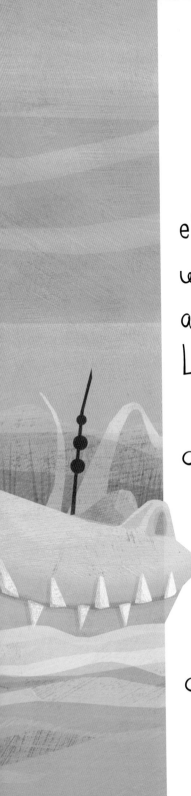

Further on, the elephant's child trod on what looked like a log at the edge of the Limpopo River.

But it was really the crocodile!

"'Scuse me, please," said the elephant's child. "Have you seen such a thing as a crocodile around here?"

The crocodile said, "I am the crocodile."

"Then will you tell me what you have for dinner?" gasped the elephant's child.

"Come close and I'll whisper," said the crocodile.

The elephant's child put his ear to the crocodile's musky tusky mouth.

At once, the crocodile caught the elephant's child by his little nose. "Today," he said, "I will begin with elephant's child!"

"Led go!" the elephant's child said, speaking through his nose. "You're hurtig be!"

Then the bi-coloured-python-rock-snake shouted, "Pull! Or you'll be in the river before you can say Jack Robinson."

The elephant's child sat back on his haunches and pulled... and his nose began to stretch.

Then the snake knotted himself
round the elephant's child's back
legs and they both pulled
together. The elephant's child's
nose grew longer and longer!

SPLASH!

At last the crocodile could pull no longer. He let go of the nose and went flailing back into the great grey-green, greasy Limpopo River.

The elephant's child wrapped his poor nose in banana leaves, and hung it in the river.

"What are you doing that for?" asked the bi-coloured-python-rock-snake.

"My nose is all out of shape," said the elephant's child. "I'm hoping it will shrink."

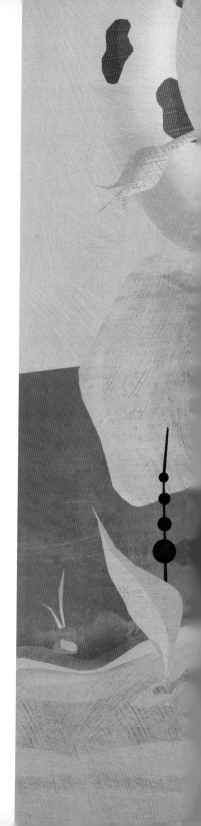

SNIFF!

Then a fly landed on the elephant's child's shoulder. He lifted up his long nose and smacked it away.

"Ah ha!" said the snake. "You couldn't have done that with a mere-smear nose."

In the afternoon, the sun shone and the elephant's child was very hot. He schlooped up some mud from the river bank and sloshed it on his head to make a trickly cool mud cap.

Splat!

"Ah ha!" said the snake again. "You couldn't have done that with a mere-smear nose."

"You're right," said the elephant's child. "I think I'll go home to all my dear family."

So the elephant's child went home, frisking and whisking his new long nose – which we now call a trunk – as he went.

When he wanted fruit to eat he pulled it down from a tree.

yank!

swish!

When flies bit him he used a branch as a swat.

do-be-do da!

And when he felt lonely he sang loudly to himself down his trunk.

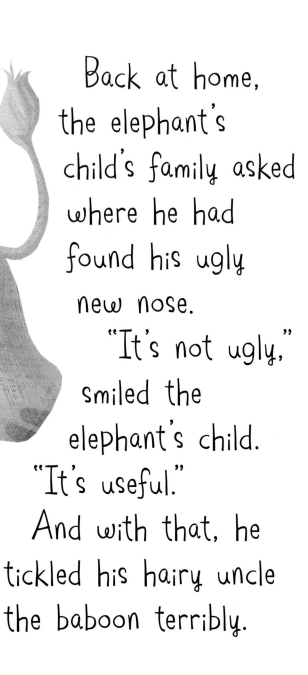

Back at home,
the elephant's
child's family asked
where he had
found his ugly
new nose.
"It's not ugly,"
smiled the
elephant's child.
"It's useful."
And with that, he
tickled his hairy uncle
the baboon terribly.

The new nose was so useful that all the elephants hurried to get new noses from the crocodile.

And ever since then, all the elephants you will ever see have noses precisely like the trunk of the 'satiable elephant's child.

The Town Mouse and the Country Mouse

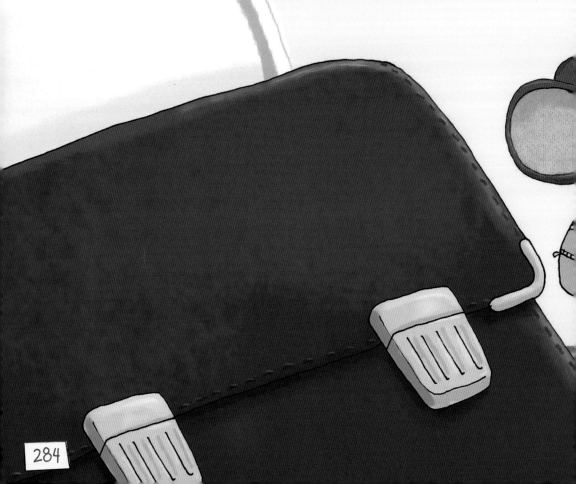

A little mouse who lived in a busy, bustling town set off on a train journey. He was going to visit his cousin in the countryside.

The mouse was excited.
He had never been out of
the city before.

285

The country mouse had been hard at work preparing for the town mouse's visit.

When the town
mouse arrived, the
cousins greeted each
other joyfully.

The country mouse showed off her home in a tree trunk. It was simple, warm and cosy.

"It's very different to my home," the town mouse said.

Once the town mouse had rested, the country mouse took him to meet the farm animals next door. They crowded round to greet him.

"Watch it!" cried the town mouse. The horse was huge, and the chicken's beak looked very sharp. The town mouse felt a little bit nervous.

That evening,
the country
mouse served
a dinner of
bread and cheese.
It was not at all like
the fancy meals the
town mouse was
used to.

All night, the
town mouse tossed
and turned in his
bed of leaves.

He was used
to sleeping in a
much softer bed.

In the morning, the town mouse asked his cousin to come and see his home. "We don't sleep on leaves in the city!" he laughed.

The country mouse agreed. She was very curious to see what a town was like.

The town mouse lived in a grand house in the middle of town. The country mouse thought it looked very smart.

The town mouse
proudly showed off
his home. It was
very comfortable.

303

The town mouse began a tour of the house. A cat prowled by while they were in the kitchen.

"Quick, hide!" squeaked the town mouse.

"Shhhhh!"

They scurried under a cup and waited, hardly daring to breathe. At last, the cat stalked away. "That was close!" said the country mouse, trembling.

Next, they crept into
the living room. There
were people there,
watching a bright,
glowing screen. The
country mouse gazed at
it — she had never seen
anything like it!

In the playroom, there were all kinds of toys. The country mouse knocked a tower of building blocks. They tumbled down around the mice.

"Yikes!" squeaked the country mouse.

309

A delicious feast was laid out on the dining room table.

There were sandwiches and pies, cakes and biscuits — everything that was good to eat. The mice began to tuck in.

"I've never had food like this before!" mumbled the country mouse.

The town mouse laughed. "This is how you could eat all the time!" he replied.

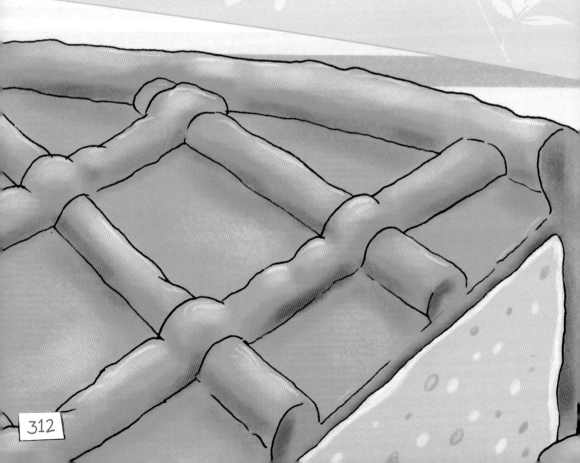

313

Suddenly, the mice heard growling and scratching at the door. Two dogs burst in, sniffing the air.

315

The dogs began to bark and jump up at the table. The mice had to run away.

Enough was enough. The country mouse decided to return to her country home at once.

"Better to live poorly in peace than richly in fear," she said.

"Goodbye!"

Little Red Riding Hood

One sunny day, Little Red Riding Hood's mother said, "Grandma is ill. Please will you take this basket of cakes and fruit to her?"

"Bye Mum!"

So Little Red Riding Hood put
on her red cape and set off.
"Don't talk to strangers,
especially if they are WOLVES!"
her mother called after her.

Little Red Riding Hood walked through the wood. The trees were tall and made scary shadows.

Suddenly, a big bad wolf jumped out.

"Where are you going?"
growled the wolf.
"I'm going to see Grandma,"
said Little Red Riding Hood.

"How sweet," said the wolf.
"Why not pick some flowers to
take to Grandma's too?"
Little Red Riding Hood
thought this was a lovely idea.

Little did she know, the big bad wolf was racing off ahead to Grandma's house while she was busy picking.

Soon the wolf was knocking softly on Grandma's door.

"It's me, Grandma," he called, trying to sound like Little Red Riding Hood. "I've brought you some cakes and fruit.

"Let me in, Grandma!"

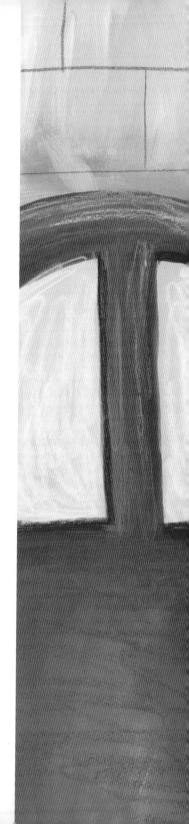

329

But Grandma wasn't silly. "That's not Little Red Riding Hood's voice," she said. She hid in the wardrobe.

"Grandma?"

No one answered the
door, so the wolf came in.

Grandma wasn't there. So the wolf put on her nightgown and bedcap and got into bed.

Soon, Little Red
Riding Hood was
knocking on the door.

"Grandma,
     it's me!"

"Come in dear,"
snarled the wolf in his
nicest voice.

"Grandma, you look odd!" said Little Red Riding Hood. "That's because I'm not very well," growled the wolf. "Come and sit beside me dear."

Little Red Riding Hood sat on the bed. "What big ears you have, Grandma," she said.

"All the better to hear you with my dear," growled the wolf.

"And what big eyes you have, Grandma," said Little Red Riding Hood, coming closer.

"All the better to see you with my dear," snarled the wolf.

"And your teeth are HUGE!" exclaimed Little Red Riding Hood. "All the better to EAT you with!" roared the wolf.

BANG BANG BANG!

He pounced, but Little Red Riding Hood screamed loudly and jumped out of reach. As the wolf leaped after her there was a loud banging at the door.

Little Red Riding Hood ran to the door and opened it.

There stood a woodcutter who had heard her screams. He raised his axe.

With a howl of fear, the big bad wolf dashed past the woodcutter, out of the cottage and away into the forest.

Then Little Red Riding Hood
heard a sound coming from
the wardrobe.

She opened the door and out tumbled Grandma, safe and sound!

"Phew!"

"I do feel better! Shall we have tea?" said Grandma. The woodcutter put the kettle on and Little Red Riding Hood got out the fruit and cakes.

"Yummy!"

Never again did Little Red Riding Hood talk to strangers. As for the wolf, he kept well away from little girls — especially those wearing red capes!

The Lion
and the
Mouse

There was once a lion who lived close to the edge of the jungle. Each day he roamed the grasslands, checking that all was well in his kingdom.

He feared no one, but everyone feared him.

The zebra mothers warned
their children about him.

"Keep your distance and all will be well."

The elephant mothers warned their children too. "I am far too big for the lion to hunt, but you are small. Stay close to me and all will be well."

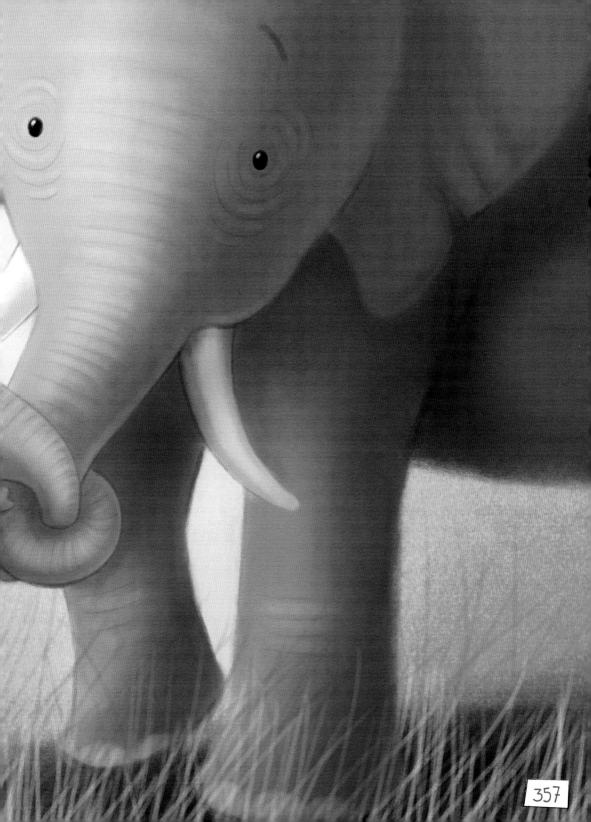

When it grew too hot during the day, the lion would walk into the jungle. It was cool and dark beneath the trees.

He would stroll along shady paths until he reached his favourite cave. There he slept for a few hours each day.

In another part of
the forest, a family of
mice had a nest in a
hole in a tree. They
were always very busy
looking for food.

One young
mouse was braver and
more curious than his
brothers and sisters.
He loved to explore.

One day, the mouse reached the edge of the jungle. He saw the great plains of grass and herds of animals.

He gasped in fear at the sight of the mighty lion on his rock, and scurried back into the jungle.

Each day, the little mouse watched the lion walking to his cave. The mouse decided that he must sneak a look inside.

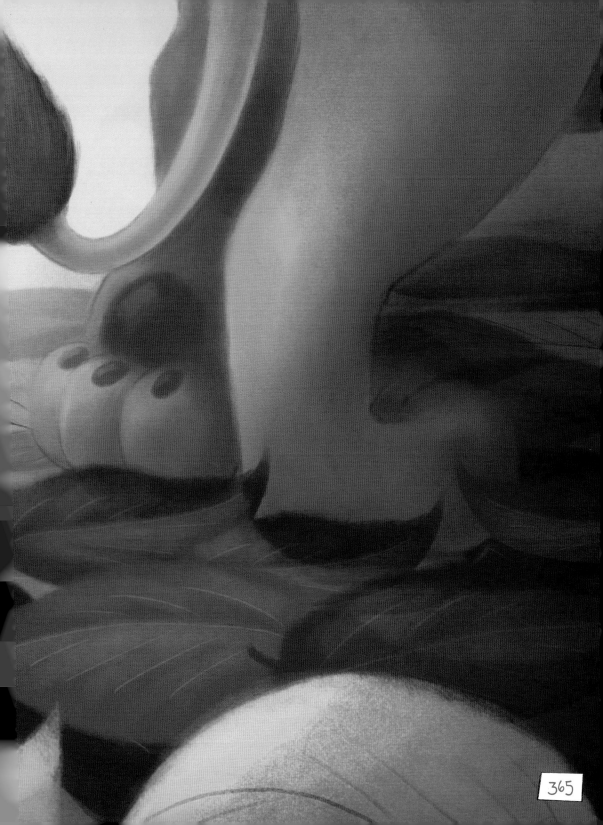

So one day, when the mouse knew the lion was on the plains, he crept through the jungle.

He sat at the mouth of the cave, trembling. Dare he go any further?

"ROAAAAR!"

A giant paw trapped the mouse. It was the lion!

"Please let me go!" squeaked the mouse. "I wasn't causing any trouble!"

369

"What are you doing here?" growled the lion.

"I was just being curious," squeaked the mouse. "Please let me go – I'll do you a good turn one day."

The lion laughed at this idea. "Well, you are brave for one so small. Off you go – and NEVER come back here again!"

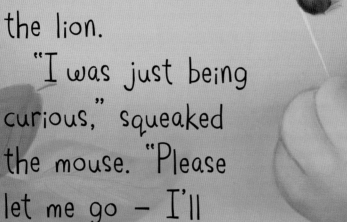

The mouse scampered away as fast as he could go.

Some weeks later, as he prowled through the jungle, the lion walked into a trap. A strong net of ropes fell on top of him.

The more the lion struggled,
the more entangled he became.
He realized the hunter
would return soon.
Exhausted, he lay still
and roared softly.

375

376

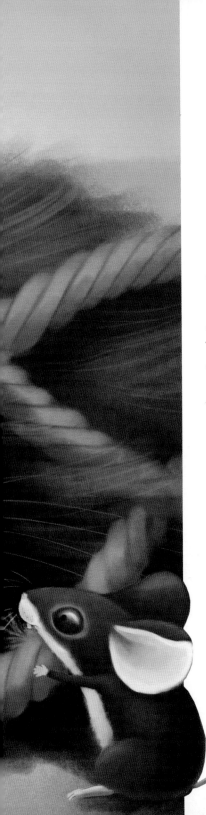

Then the lion saw a tiny creature standing in front of him. It was the mouse.

"Let me help you," squeaked the mouse, and he set to work gnawing the rope.

Before long, the lion gave a mighty shake and the gnawed ropes fell to the ground.

The mouse found himself scooped up in a giant paw. "Thank you," growled the lion.

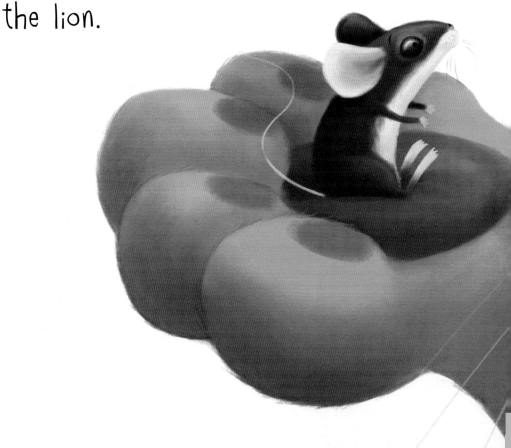

379

Then the lion placed the mouse on his back. "Hold on to my mane," he instructed.

Suddenly they were racing through the jungle.

The mouse held on tight, his eyes squeezed shut.

381

The lion arrived at the grassy plain and gave a mighty roar!